The Last Stand Of A Queen

Verses Kindler Publication

Verses Kindler Publication.

Website: www.verseskindlerpublication.com

The Last Stand Of A Queen

By: Ms. Biniza .F. Wadia

ISBN: 978-93-49532-91-5

FICTION STORIES 1st Edition

Price: INR 249/$13

Disclaimer

The Last Stand Of A Queen is written by Ms. Biniza .F. Wadia. The entirety of this published work comprises the original content of the author, who has undertaken diligent efforts in its editing. The characters depicted herein may be fictitious or inspired by real events; however, they are not intended to cause offense or represent any prejudice against any caste or system. Any similarity to the names of actual individuals, locations, or institutions is purely coincidental and serves the narrative. The author bears sole responsibility for the originality of this work; the publisher assumes no liability thereof.

Index

About the Book

This book takes you deep into the life of Rani Lakshmibai, the fearless Queen of Jhansi who stood against British rule during the Indian Rebellion of 1857. It reveals powerful and lesser-known stories about her childhood, inner strength, struggles, and the choices that shaped her journey as a warrior and leader.

You will see her not only as a queen but as a human being who faced heartbreak, loss, and overwhelming odds with unshakable courage. Through vivid storytelling, the book brings her world to life, showing how her actions became a symbol of bravery and freedom.

At the heart of this narrative is a call to every young woman who carries the spirit of Lakshmibai within her. Jhansi ki Rani is the flame that flickers in every heart that refuses to bow, the battle cry in every woman who rises, unshaken and unafraid.

About the Author

Hello!

My name is Biniza Wadia. I am twelve years old, and I love stories. I enjoy reading them, watching them, and most of all, writing them.

Ever since I first learned how to write, I have been filling notebooks with my ideas. I love exploring history, imagining inspiring characters, and dreaming up big adventures. Writing has always been my way of understanding the world and seeing it in new and exciting ways.

I live with my family, which includes my parents, my grandparents, and our fluffy dog named Blacky. Blacky often ends up sitting right outside our entrance door like a quiet little muse. Somehow, he always inspires me to write even more.

My room is filled with books, sketchpads, and all sorts of colourful pens. History books are my favourite because I enjoy learning about people who have done great things for humanity and my country. Their stories inspire me deeply.

School is fun most of the time, and my favourite subject is English. I am also learning how to paint, although I am still working on taking my creativity to the next level.

When I'm not writing or reading, I'm usually studying German, spending time with my parents, or watching my favorite cartoons.

Some people say I am quiet, and that is true. But just because I am silent does not mean I am not thinking about amazing things. Even when I sit by a window and watch the rain, my imagination remains wide awake.

I hope that through this book, you feel inspired by the legend and the world, just like I was.

Thank you for joining me on this journey through history.

CHAPTER ONE: WHY I CHOSE RANI LAXMIBAI

Dear Reader,

When I first came across some little known facts about Rani Laxmibai, I knew that more people needed to know them. That is why I started my book. That is why I picked Rani Laxmibai. She is not just a queen from history, she is a real hero who fought for her people and stood up for what was right, even when everything seemed impossible.

We hear a lot about kings, generals, and famous battles, but amazing women like Rani Laxmibai do not always get the same spotlight, even though they deserve it just as much. It made me wonder why their stories are not told as often. Women like her showed just as much bravery, leadership, and strength as the men we always read about. Sometimes they even had to work twice as hard to be taken seriously. I think it is really unfair that their courage is not shared more.

When I learned about how Rani Laxmibai fought for her kingdom and never gave up, even when she was facing huge armies, it made me feel even more proud to write about her. She showed that women can be fierce warriors, smart leaders, and strong voices for freedom. I believe that if more people knew about her and others like her, it would change how we look at history.

Rani Laxmibai was born in 1828 and grew up learning how to ride horses, use swords, and fight like a warrior. That was very unusual for girls at that time, but she did not care about what people expected. She just did what she loved. Later, when she became the queen of Jhansi, she did not just sit on a throne and wear pretty clothes. She worked hard to protect her kingdom, and when the British tried to take over, she refused to give up without a fight.

What made me admire her even more was how she fought side by side with her soldiers. She did not just give orders from far away. She was right there in the middle of the battle, riding on horseback with her toddler son tied to her back. That image stayed with me because it shows just how brave and fierce she really was. She fought not just for herself, but for her people, for her country, and for the idea of freedom.

I also found out that after the British tried to annex Jhansi unfairly, Rani Laxmibai tried every peaceful way first to solve the problem. Only when they refused to listen did she choose to fight. That shows she was wise and thoughtful too, not just brave but smart and fair.

As I was writing this book, it dawned on me how crucial it is for more individuals to find out about women like her. Many queens, leaders, and freedom fighters accomplished extraordinary feats, yet their stories are not sufficiently told. Sometimes it seems as if history overlooks them, despite the fact that they were just as brave, intelligent, and significant as the men we always hear about.

Their names get hidden under all the stories about kings and wars, and that is not fair. It is not because they did not do enough, but because people did not think their stories mattered as much, and that needs to change.

Rani Laxmibai deserves to be remembered, and not just remembered, celebrated. She should be talked about in classrooms, written about in books, and honored the same way the famous kings and generals are. By learning and sharing her story, we are making sure her bravery and sacrifices are never forgotten. I believe that when we give more attention to women like Rani Laxmibai, we show the world that true courage has no gender, and that leadership and strength belong to everyone.

I really enjoyed doing my research for this project. Every time I found a new piece of information about her, I felt even more inspired. It made me want to be braver in my own life, to speak up when something is wrong, and to never back down just because something is hard.

I hope that when people read my book, they feel curious and excited to learn more too. Learning about Rani Laxmibai made me realize that history is not just a bunch of dates and facts, it is full of real people who lived amazing lives and made a difference. I hope that after reading about her, others will want to do their own research, not just about Rani Laxmibai, but about other amazing women leaders from history too.

If you want to start, you do not have to find a huge textbook. You can look for small articles, watch videos, or even visit your local library and ask for help finding books about different freedom fighters and queens. Sometimes just reading a few interesting facts can pull you into a whole new story you never knew before. It is like being a detective, except you are discovering real heroes.

I think if more kids my age got interested in history, we would all see that there are so many people who paved the way for the world we live in today. It would also show us that leaders come from everywhere, and that bravery and strength are not only found in famous names we always hear about. If more people knew these stories, I think the world would be even more inspired and stronger, because we would all understand that anyone can make a difference, no matter how young or old, and no matter where they come from.

Doing this project made me fall in love with history a little more, and I hope it does the same for everyone who reads my book.

Rani Laxmibai will always be my queen of choice, not just because she was a queen, but because she was a real hero.

I hope this book helps more people learn about Rani Laxmibai and everything she did. She was so brave, smart, and determined, and I think her story deserves to be told to everyone, not just in history books but in everyday conversations too. I hope after reading this, you feel inspired to find out even more about her, because there is so much more to her life than I could fit here. Maybe you will even discover other amazing women from history who made a difference too. If we keep learning and sharing their stories, we can make sure they are never forgotten.

With Love And Endless Curiosity,

Biniza

CHAPTER TWO: BEFORE SHE WAS RANI

In the old city of Varanasi—where the Ganges flows like a prayer along the spine of India—a girl called Manikarnika Tambe was born. At home, she was called Manu, a name gentle on the tongue, as if the burden of destiny had not yet fallen upon her shoulders.

The precise birth year of Manikarnika Tambe is a matter of historical controversy. British accounts indicate 1827, whereas Indian sources, based on oral traditions and nationalist literature, tend to quote 1835. However, one sure thing is the location of her birth: Varanasi, a major cultural and religious hub of India at the time. The city, nestled in the arms of the holy Ganges, was a meeting point of learning, piety, and rebellion, a fitting place for a child who would come to represent all three.

The astrologers reckoned that her birth would be prophesied as the alignment of Pantheon stars, revealing infinite potential and godly splendour. The child, they said, would carry within her the essence of the three great goddesses of the Hindu pantheon—Lakshmi, the blithe deity of prosperity; Durga, the fierce protector and symbol of power; and Saraswati, the wise muse of art and knowledge.

At the beginning of the 19th Century, India was languidly suffering, crippled by displacement, and bowing to alien tyranny. During this period, India was infested with fractured kingdoms blended with smouldering resistance—nothing less than a fertile land for the British East India Company. The company's influence expanded onto the subcontinent's circulatory systems and didn't shy away from deceit and manipulation as a mode of capturing it.

It was not yet a crown colony, but it was a hunted land, sold off in pieces by those who feared war or courted favour.

Manikarnika's father, Moropant Tambe, was a court advisor in Bithoor during the reign of the Peshwa in the Maratha Empire; he was a man stripped of his position yet richly cultured and prideful. Her mother, Bhagirathi, passed away when Manikarnika was still very young.

The household of the Peshwa was not quite ordinary – it served as both a sanctuary and a remnant of the Maratha pride that had once dominated a significant part of India. Unlike most girls born during her time, Manu did not have to navigate the suffocatingly restricted world expected of girls during this period. Instead, she benefited from the robust culture of the Peshwa's court, which included nurturing martial and intellectual undertakings.

The Peshwa, who had no children, did lavish affection upon her and raised her like a daughter. It is said hitherto that she became very close with some of the other young ones in the court, including but not limited to Nana Sahib, the Peshwa's adopted son, and Tatya Tope, who was a family friend and a military tutor. These boys would become essential leaders in the Indian Rebellion of 1857, but long before that, they were just playmates and co-pilots in training – equals on the riding grounds and off the horses.

Childless and fond of Manu's spirit, the Peshwa treated her like a daughter. According to legend, she formed close bonds with other children in the court, especially Nana Sahib, the Peshwa's adopted son, and Tatya Tope, a family friend and military mentor. These boys would later become key figures in the Indian Rebellion of 1857, but long before that, they were simply playmates and partners in training—equals in the courtyard and on horseback.

Unlike many girls of her time, confined to domestic arts and devotional education, Manu welcomed an unconventional upbringing. She studied to read and write fluently in Marathi, Sanskrit, and some Persian, gaining exposure to religious texts and military chronicles. She was immersed in the great epics of Ramayana and Mahabharata for their strategy, integrity, and dharma lessons.

Her physical conditioning was equally impressive. Manu learned horse riding, sword fighting, archery, and marksmanship with court tutors under close observation. She excelled at carrying weapons, riding fearlessly aboard powerful steeds, and undergoing military training with an air of confidence, often outpacing her male friends.

Those who observed her praised her sharp mind, determination, and unwavering focus. Even as a child, she was spirited, disciplined, and fiercely intelligent. A quiet life did not seem to be her destiny.

Before 1857, not much is known about Rani Lakshmibai's life. Today, she is regarded as a fearless fighter who galloped into battle with her baby son strapped to her back, defying the British Empire.

However, life is oddly hidden in the shadows behind this famous picture. There is a patchwork of conjecture, oral tradition, and fragmentary accounts surrounding the years leading up to her transformation into the Rani of Jhansi, including her early years, formative experiences, and entry into royal life. First-person records, letters, and diaries—anything that could have preserved her inner world—are conspicuously missing. The lens of admiration and resistance that subsequent generations applied to her memory shapes a large portion of our beliefs about her early life rather than concrete evidence.

Numerous academics and authors have tried to identify the features of her early years. During the last years of British rule, she became a nationalist icon and her youth was romanticized in Vrindavan Lal Verma's semi-fictional novel Jhansi ki Rani (1946). Written from a feminist perspective, Mahasweta Devi's Laxmibai highlighted the difficulties she encountered as a powerful woman. However, rather than being purely historical, both works are interpretive.

The works of British colonial historians such as John Kaye and Thomas R. Metcalfe referred to Lakshmibai. Rather, they mainly focused on her military actions during the rebellion, portraying her as either a tragic figure or a dangerous rebel. They hardly ever acknowledged her intelligence, political savvy, or early life.

Scholars like Tapti Roy have adopted a more scholarly stance in recent decades, assembling a more complete picture through oral histories, court archives, and regional records. Even so, their efforts illustrate the limited amount of source material.

Historian Joyce Lebra undertook extensive research and published The Rani of Jhansi: A Study in Female Heroism in India in 1986. Lebra sifted through court records, military dispatches, and local histories to separate legend from likelihood.

Even earlier, Marathi writer and nationalist Vishnu Bhatt Godshe penned his firsthand account of the 1857 uprising in Majha Pravas ("My Travels"), where he briefly mentioned the Rani. Though not focused on her early life, the work is a rare contemporary reference. Likewise, Subhadra Kumari Chauhan's stirring Hindi poem Jhansi ki Rani (the famous "Khoob ladi mardani..." lines) reinforced her image in the popular imagination, though again with more emotion than accuracy. Even if not much is known about her early life, her later life shaped the history of India.

CHAPTER THREE: THE MAKING OF A WARRIOR

There are lives formed by inheritance and others by interruption, by sudden and unexpected events that disrupt one's life. The latter formed Manikarnika Tambe's early life.

Not by ease nor ceremony but by rupture.

Women vanished in obscurity; men in flames. Manu fell between both: too little to command respect and too quick to be ignored. Her world, which had once smelled of sandalwood and rice, now reeked of the iron smell of discipline.

Loss does not always come with thunder. Sometimes, it comes to a child as quiet as a shadow—uninvited, permanent, and silent. Her mother's arms, once a source of comfort, now transformed into sword hilts, a symbol of her new identity. What had been lullabies were now the pulsating hoofbeats. Her laughter, once a symbol of innocence, gradually gave way to the silence of a young warrior, a testament to the loss of her childhood.

When Manikarnika Tambe's mother, Bhagirathi, died, the silence within the house uttered more than the most elegy of funeral mantras could. The world didn't slow. The prayers were sung, the lamps lit—but the softness was lost. Something hard and strange grew in its stead. The girl who used to grasp her mother's hand grasped a sword now.

Mourning came early and with clarity. Even at eight or nine, Manu knew girls were treated differently regarding sorrow. She was supposed to cry silently, to withdraw into submission. But she became acuter. Her eyes had started to pick up on what others were glossing over: the quivering in a widow's voice, the hesitation of servants when the British were spoken of, the wearied expression in her father's eyes when he tucked away yet another letter from the court.

She was not born with a crown or a destiny—but she was born watching a world where women disappeared too quickly. That, she decided, would not be her story.

Her questions became louder. When a priest explained the Ramayana, she interrupted to ask why Sita was abandoned. When her tutor spoke of valiant kings, she asked for names of warrior queens. When no one answered, she searched the scrolls herself. She read about Ahilyabai Holkar, Razia Sultan, and legends passed from woman to woman, often in whispers. Her reading was not for leisure—it was for survival.

She was granted freedom at Bithoor Peshwa's court, but freedom had boundaries. Her closest friends—Nana Sahib and Tatya Tope—were instructed on how to rule and order. She was urged to study, but always in moderation. A girl with an excess of knowledge was referred to as arrogant. A girl with a sword was referred to as dangerous. Nevertheless, she went on.

One afternoon, a visiting British officer was in the children's practice. "The girl is courageous," he grumbled, observing her splitting a clay pot with one arrow. But she will grow up soon."

Manu caught him. She didn't waver. She grabbed her second arrow and struck the next target—cleaner, quicker, dead on. The message was unmistakable: she wasn't here to impress. She was here to train.

She was ten years old. Her first real lesson in injustice did not come from war—it came from silence.

A girl from the court, almost as young as Manu, was wedded and a widow within a year. She returned dressed in white robes, not allowed to smile, eat sweets, or participate in rituals. The court neglected her. Manu asked them why the girl was being condemned for staying alive, and they replied, "That is our way."

"Our path is broken," Manu whispered softly. "We simply do not wish to mend it." From that point on, she insisted on being more than just a student of tradition. She would study it, sure—but only to rework it.

Her training became more rigorous. She got up before dawn and sparred till evening. She practised blindfolded to sharpen her senses. She read war chronicles and started maintaining a diary where she wrote down quotes from the Gita and her comments. One of them read: "A warrior fights not for hatred, but to protect those who cannot fight. Strength is not how loud you speak—but how long your silence can endure before you must act." It was said she could mount a galloping horse without reins and that her arrow could split a mango mid-flight. But it wasn't these feats that defined her. It was how she carried herself after—quiet, confident, and hungry for the next lesson.

Not all her battles were physical. Some were political, some cultural. She questioned why soldiers bowed to corrupt ministers, why British men gave orders in Indian courts, and why treaties meant to protect kingdoms were used to steal them. Her father, Moropant, warned her: "Speak too boldly, and you'll be silenced." He cared for her but was wary of the world's indifference toward bold women. "You speak like a woman who expects the world to listen," he said. "But the world rarely does." Manu met his gaze with a determined look and replied, "Then I will speak louder."

At that point, Manu had already made a promise to herself. If the world punished her for speaking up, then silence would be the first war she'd win.

It was also during this period that she started dreaming about fire—not symbolic fire—actual fire. Cities blazed in her fantasies, flags ripped in the wind, and horse riders rode beneath skies rent apart by cannon smoke. But rather than inducing fear, the fantasies invigorated her. She would rise before daylight, pulses pounding as though called by something beyond her control.

She started noticing omens everywhere. A snake that passed in front of her without biting. A kite that would not come down. A coin found with the face of a long-forgotten queen. Some believed she was dreaming up omens; others thought the gods were eyeing her. Manu believed neither entirely. But she believed in preparedness.

She was still technically a child, but only by the calendar. Emotionally, intellectually, and spiritually, she had passed over. She had grieved, questioned, and trained. The purpose was all that was left, and it came sooner than she had anticipated.

The rumours started when she was barely a teenager—rumours of marriage matches, royal matrimony, and the traditional responsibilities given to girls. But Manu had terms. If she were to marry, it would not be into submission. It would be into battle.

When Jhansi made the offer, her instructors instructed her to remain quiet and demure. She smiled graciously and asked, "Does the prince have a finer sword than mine?"

Laughter came next. Her question, though, was profound.

She was yet to be wed or wear a coronet.

The British had not yet heard her name.

But the warrior already existed— sculpted not by bloodshed but by an infinite sea of bold refusals:

To remain mute, diminish one's dreams, or embrace society's fate without question.

So when some whispers of "Jhansi" reached the court, she was prepared.

Prepared not only to govern but to take charge.

Not for the reason of her being labelled as courageous,

which someone told her, but rather the truth -

she had already accomplished that.

The world would one day know her as Rani Lakshmibai.

But she had transformed into a warrior long before receiving the crown.

The rains that year came late, and the air was arid. Bad news came from Delhi and Bengal: Another tiny kingdom was absorbed, and another treaty was violated. The British were closing their grip, and Indian leaders pondered resisting or surviving.

Manikarnika had already made her decision. She would not wait to be granted freedom. She would grow into it—blade by blade, breath by breath, vow by vow. And the world would soon call her *Rani Lakshmibai.*

But long before the crown touched her head, the warrior had already risen.

CHAPTER FOUR: THE ROYAL MARRIAGE

The rains had barely returned to Bithoor when the proposal arrived—carried not on the back of a horse or the fold of a royal decree but in the softened tones of elders speaking around doorframes, never directly. She heard it first not as an announcement but as a change in the air—like the pause before an arrow is released.

Manikarnika, no longer the child sparring under sunrise or questioning rituals in a whisper, listened with a calm that surprised even her father. The fires of training still burned behind her eyes, but the world was shifting again—this time, not through loss or resistance but through choice.

The warrior had been shaped in silence. Now, she was being summoned into visibility.

Not to vanish behind a veil but to step into the light of statecraft.

The match was with Jhansi—an old kingdom with a tired monarch and a future clouded by British designs. Most saw a title. She saw a frontier. This was not a surrender to tradition. It was a redirection of strength. A battlefield of a different kind. She crossed into Jhansi without fanfare. Her chariot bore no extravagant silks, no perfumed heralds. She carried fewer ornaments than expected of a new queen but more presence than anyone anticipated. In her eyes was a stillness shaped by years of preparation and in her posture, a resolve that no crown could gift.

Raja Gangadhar Rao was not the image she had painted in her imagination. He was older, quieter, and wrapped in a layer of weariness that came from ruling a kingdom under siege—not from battle but from bureaucracy. He had seen allies turn uncertain, treaties crumble, and sovereign pride auctioned off to foreign hands in velvet gloves.

When they met, it was not with a gaze of romance or ownership. It was something else—something rarer—recognition.

She did not bow too profoundly. He did not patronize.

He asked if she had any fears. She wondered if he still had a loyal cavalry.

The alliance was sealed with rituals, yes, but more truly in the understanding that both were stepping into a shared solitude—one of duty, of dwindling autonomy, of futures negotiated in the shadow of an empire. Their wedding was not a culmination; it was a beginning—a recalibration of purpose.

Her name changed that day—from Manikarnika to Lakshmibai. But it was not a loss of identity. It was a layering, a stepping stone across the river of transformation.

In the following weeks, the palace learned quickly that this queen was not ornamental.

She began with observation. She walked the corridors quietly, speaking little but listening deeply. She mapped the fort's architecture and noted the cracks in both stone and morale. She rode through the city disguised as a local, ears open to grievances that never reached the durbar.

She did not seek to replace tradition but to sharpen it. Her education expanded beyond epics and ethics to include land revenue codes, military structures, treaties, and the tangled language of the Company's legal scrolls. She wanted to understand the tools used to conquer—not to fear them, but to wield them if she must.

To his credit, the Raja gave her space. He had married a queen by name but found himself standing beside a strategist by spirit. She challenged his ministers, questioned obsolete customs, and wrote letters in her hand. She made herself impossible to exclude.

And yet, she carried herself with grace—never brash, never loud. Only deliberate. As though each word she chose carried the weight of her lineage and the warning of her legacy.

The people of Jhansi began to shift in their whispers. "The girl is not like the queens before," some said. "She walks like one born of battle, not to be served." Soldiers nodded when she passed. Young women looked longer than they were allowed.

She became a symbol without ever intending to. Her presence alone disrupted what was expected of a royal bride. Not because she demanded it—but because she refused to diminish.

And through all of it, Raja Gangadhar Rao watched—not with suspicion, but a certain reverence. He had lost much in life—first love, stability, control over his land. But here was a queen who carried loss not as a burden but as fuel. She did not decorate his palace. She fortified it.

Their conversations were never public. But amid open scrolls and half-drunk cups of tea in the quiet of twilight, they discussed the shape of coming storms.

The British had not yet knocked directly on Jhansi's gate. But their presence curled at its edges, like smoke from a fire still distant, but specific.

Lakshmibai felt it in her bones. In the letters with foreign signatures. In the delayed payments. She read the clause-ridden contracts late into the night while the rest of the palace slept.

She was still young—barely fifteen. But she knew history did not wait for permission to unfold. And she was done waiting to be called brave. She had been brave long before titles and ceremonies.

And now, as the queen of Jhansi, she did not plan to rule quietly.

CHAPTER FIVE: A KINGDOM CALLED JHANSI

Jhansi, a city characterized not by its size but by the tenacity of its citizens and the legacy of its rulers, throbbed with quiet strength long before treaties were broken and conflicts took shape. Lakshmibai arrived in this convoluted and legendary land as a student of power rather than as a symbol.

She entered by observation rather than with fanfare. Her gaze lifted to the walls of the fort that had withstood generations of transformation as her feet touched the red earth of her new home. Yes, it was stone but also expectation, resistance, and memory.

From her first days in Jhansi, it became clear that this was not a city that wore its politics loudly. Its strength was more subterranean—woven into the markets, in the discipline of its soldiers, and in the measured rhythm of the durbar. It was here that Lakshmibai would witness what it meant to lead, not through bloodlines or rituals but through resilience and clarity.

Maharaja Gangadhar Rao, her husband, governed with wisdom and compassion. He had become king in 1843, succeeding a kingdom torn apart by internal chaos and cautious British tutelage. The East India Company's expanding taste for annexation had earlier interfered with the administration of Jhansi. But Gangadhar Rao, methodical and educated, brought order through reform.

A cultured man, the Maharaja was fond of books and devoted to tradition.

He read Marathi, Persian, and Sanskrit with ease and had a palace library full of precious manuscripts—scriptures, medical texts, poetry, and political theory. His court became a sanctuary of stability in a region fractured by colonial intrigue, politics, and declining princely power.

Lakshmibai quickly noticed that his rule was marked by subtle strength. He did not govern by fear. Instead, he governed by foresight. He encouraged open dialogue with his ministers and promoted local governance through trusted administrators. Under his watch, revenue collection was restructured, unfair taxation curtailed, and local agriculture strengthened through irrigation and land reforms.

Gangadhar Rao stood out most in how he held his ground against British interference. Though always diplomatic in tone, he was firm in content. He insisted on the autonomy promised to Jhansi through earlier treaties and resisted any amendments that weakened his court's sovereignty. Here, Lakshmibai first witnessed the quiet balancing act between royal duty and imperial diplomacy—how one could outwardly comply while inwardly preserving principle.

She observed his every move, often silent in the durbar, seated beside him or slightly behind. But what she absorbed was profound: the art of listening with intent, the weight of a pause before speaking, decisions that protected not just people but their dignity, and how governance could be an act of stewardship, not command.

Despite the peace he maintained, she saw the worry behind his eyes. Gangadhar Rao had no surviving heir. The East India Company had begun applying Lord Dalhousie's Doctrine of Lapse, which allowed them to annex any kingdom without a direct biological successor. The Maharaja knew Jhansi's fate could hinge on that single detail.

In 1851, a son was born to Lakshmibai and the Maharaja. He was named Damodar Rao. The palace rejoiced, but fate struck quickly and cruelly—the child passed away in infancy. Lakshmibai, still a teenager, experienced motherhood and mourning in a single breath.

Two years later, in 1853, with his health failing, Gangadhar Rao formally adopted a relative's son, Anand Rao, and renamed him Damodar Rao. The ceremony was not private. It was conducted before a British political officer, and a written declaration followed—petitioning that the boy be recognized as the legitimate heir and that Lakshmibai be appointed regent should anything happen to the Maharaja.

In Indian law and custom, adoption was valid. However, the British East India Company had little interest in customs. When Gangadhar Rao died in late 1853, a letter came from Calcutta: Jhansi would be annexed. The Doctrine of Lapse was invoked. The adopted child was not recognized. The throne was considered vacant.

Lakshmibai, still wearing the white robes of mourning, stood before the British officer and reportedly declared: "I shall not surrender my Jhansi." But she did not rush to arms. She petitioned. She argued. She appealed directly to Lord Dalhousie and later to London. She laid out legal documents, historical precedents, and moral arguments with the clarity of someone who had learned not just what justice looked like—but how to defend it precisely.

They ignored her.

But they underestimated her.

Through those early years in Jhansi, Lakshmibai had quietly and systematically transformed from a royal bride into a masterful reader of political terrain. Watching Gangadhar Rao taught her the power of composed leadership, aligning vision with action, and honouring the past while preparing for storms ahead.

She had seen how a good ruler didn't just protect the land—they preserved the people's trust. Gangadhar Rao had done that. And now, as that trust was betrayed by external hands, Lakshmibai was not mourning a lost title—she was preparing to protect the legacy he left behind.

And it wasn't just about a throne.

It was about Jhansi—a city she had grown to understand not as a possession but as a living memory, a living promise.

When they dismissed her petitions and tried to strip her of her place, they thought they were silencing a widow.

They were, instead, igniting a queen.

CHAPTER SIX: LOSS AFTER LOSS

The palace had never been so quiet.

Where once music spilled into the courtyards and light danced through latticed windows, now only the echo of footsteps remained—soft, hesitant, respectful of a grief too vast to name. Jhansi, a city of fortitude and legacy, stood still as its queen faced sorrow that no crown could ease.

In 1851, after years of yearning and anticipation, Rani Lakshmibai and Maharaja Gangadhar Rao welcomed their son into the world. They named him Damodar Rao, and the palace sensed younger and brighter for a fleeting season. The birth of an heir had not only given personal joy—it had ensured continuity for the throne, stability for the people, and reassurance against British scrutiny.

But that comfort dissolved cruelly. Within a few months, Damodar Rao fell gravely ill. No remedy, no prayer, no court physician could reverse what fate had sealed. He died in infancy, leaving his mother hollowed, his father subdued. Lakshmibai, not yet twenty, wrapped her son's lifeless form herself. The palace corridors bore no cries—only silence, unrelenting and raw.

The child's death was more than personal—it reopened old wounds and exposed political danger. Gangadhar Rao, already weakened by illness and years of rule under British shadow, grew visibly frailer. With its Doctrine of Lapse looming like a storm cloud, the British East India Company saw opportunity in every royal vulnerability.

By 1853, it was clear the Maharaja's health was declining. Every court session, every dispatch he signed, was underscored by the awareness that time was slipping. Lakshmibai remained by his side—not only as wife and consort, but as counselor, listener, and witness. Together, they discussed what must come next.

On November 20, 1853, Gangadhar Rao adopted his cousin's son, Anand Rao, in a formal ceremony. The boy was renamed Damodar Rao in memory of the child they had lost. The adoption, conducted in the presence of a British political officer, was meticulously documented. A letter accompanied the event, addressed to the British government, requesting that Damodar Rao be recognized as the legal heir and that Lakshmibai serve as regent if anything happened to the Maharaja.

It was not sentiment—it was strategy.

The very next day, Gangadhar Rao died. Jhansi plunged into mourning. Rituals were performed, the pyre lit, and the widow cloaked in white. But Lakshmibai did not retreat. Even in mourning, she remained alert. Grief did not render her passive; it refined her purpose.

Yet the British response was cold and calculated. Lord Dalhousie, Governor-General of India, rejected the adoption under the Doctrine of Lapse. He declared the child illegitimate for succession and pronounced Jhansi annexed by the British.

A kingdom taken. A will ignored. A queen insulted.

Lakshmibai responded with dignity and legal precision. She drafted formal appeals, citing Indian custom and prior precedent. She wrote directly to the Governor-General, then to officials in Calcutta, and finally to representatives of the Crown in London. Her letters were elegant, reasoned, and firm. She reminded them of the promise to Indian rulers that sovereignty would be respected. She called for justice—not for herself, but for Jhansi.

Every letter was refused, and every appeal was unanswered. Behind their legal language lay a clear truth: they wanted Jhansi, and they did not care how they took it.

But they had miscalculated one thing—they believed Lakshmibai would yield.

Instead, she rose.

She began reorganizing the court, ensuring the administration remained loyal and intact. She brought in trusted advisors and reviewed the state's finances, logistics, and military capacity. Quietly, steadily, she started forming a defense—not rebellion—yet—but resistance, rooted in preparation.

The people of Jhansi watched with reverence. This was not a queen retreating into the shadows of widowhood. This was a woman who had suffered the loss of her child, her husband, and her crown—yet stood taller with each blow.

Behind closed doors, she trained, reviewed maps, walked the ramparts, read histories of past uprisings, and paid special attention to how rulers fell—not through weakness but hesitation. The world might have tried to fold her into silence, but she refused. Instead, she carved from her grief a sense of invincibility.

Still, she grieved.

There were nights she wept alone, the palace hushed but never truly asleep. Her hand would rest on the cradle that once held her son, now an artifact of memory. The royal chambers, now empty of laughter, echoed only with resolve.

And yet, even in that sorrow, she remained vigilant. She remembered her husband's calm counsel, measured voice in court, and belief in reason over rage. She held those lessons tightly, not as relics of a lost era but as blueprints for what she must now become.

In public, she was stately. In private, she was steel.

When 1857 arrived and rebellion spread across the Indian subcontinent, it did not surprise her. The soil had long been seeded with discontent. But what she chose to do next became legend.

The Rani who had endured loss after loss did not simply react. She led.

But it was in these earlier moments—between death and denial, between petitions and betrayal—that the transformation took place—not on the battlefield but in the quiet aftermath of devastation.

This was the moment everything changed.

Grief has many faces—some loud, others quiet. But for Lakshmibai, grief became the forge in which her resolve was tempered. In two years, she had lost a son, a husband, and a throne. Yet what she refused to lose was her will.

She did not simply endure tragedy—she absorbed it, studied it, and turned it into power. What the world tried to take from her, she reclaimed through courage. Instead, what was meant to silence her became the start of her voice echoing across a wounded empire.

This was no longer the story of a queen who ruled from a throne. This was now the rise of a warrior who would defend her people from the front lines.

In the wake of every loss, she found something unshakable within herself.

And though the empire had taken much, it had not taken everything.

Because in that quiet, life-altering moment, Lakshmibai was no longer waiting to lead.

She had already begun.

CHAPTER SEVEN: THE BRITISH SAY NO

The ink had barely dried on the mourning cloths. The embers of Gangadhar Rao's funeral pyre still glowed faintly in the memory of Jhansi's people. Yet even before the kingdom had time to grieve appropriately, the East India Company struck its blow. The Doctrine of Lapse—cold, impersonal, legal—descended upon Jhansi like a judgment already written in stone.

The British said no.

No to the adopted son.

No to the letter signed in the presence of their political agent.

No to the ancient customs of inheritance and succession.

They said no to the woman left behind with a child in her arms and a nation at her feet.

It was not just a denial of legality—it was a denial of dignity.

When the official letter arrived, it bore the formality of empire, not its conscience. It declared that the dictates of policy would annex Jhansi. That Lakshmibai, now widowed, had no legal standing to rule. That her adopted son, Damodar Rao, was not recognized as heir. That the throne she had supported, advised, and preserved—was no longer hers.

But Lakshmibai was no longer a figure who could be erased with ink.

She had stood beside a king and watched empires manoeuvre. She had walked through grief and emerged without fear. Now, she stood at the threshold of history, and when the British said no—she did not bow her head.

She lifted it.

The first thing she did was write.

She drafted petitions in impeccable, formal Marathi and English, addressed to Governor-General Lord Dalhousie and forwarded to the British authorities in Calcutta. In them, she detailed the adoption ceremony, the presence of the British representative, and the customs that had long governed Indian monarchies. Her argument was not emotional but constitutional, sharp, and dignified.

There were no demands, only facts. There was no anger, only the insistence that justice be honoured.

But every letter was ignored. Every plea returned void.

Behind the silence lay the truth: Jhansi was not a legal question. It was a political calculation. The British wanted a stronger hold on Bundelkhand. Jhansi's annexation fit their map better than its independence.

Lakshmibai understood this. But she also understood something far more vital—her people were watching.

The palace no longer rang with royal decrees, but the city's pulse had begun to beat faster. In marketplaces and temples, in the shaded courtyards of nobles and the thatched huts of farmers, the same question stirred: Would the Rani step back—or would she stand up?

She chose the latter.

In 1854, she was ordered to vacate the palace and accept a pension. A quiet life was offered—modest, managed, and away from power.

She declined.

Not in violence. Not yet.

She moved to the Rani Mahal, a smaller palace, and began to act—not as a former queen but as a guardian of a stolen inheritance. She lived modestly but not invisibly. She began assembling an administrative council, discreetly meeting with military officers still loyal to Jhansi and continued educating Damodar Rao in the traditions and obligations of kingship.

She would not allow her son to grow up in a world where he might erased right.

More than that, she began walking through the lanes of Jhansi—not as royalty but as kin. She spoke to shopkeepers, listened to farmers, and visited local shrines. And wherever she walked, the message spread like flame: The Rani has not yielded. She spoke little in public, but her presence was enough. The people began training again—quietly. Former soldiers who had served under the Maharaja started returning to the city. Blacksmiths resumed sharpening old blades.

Maps were drawn. Stockpiles of food and weapons began to gather in storerooms beneath the fort.

She was building a resistance—but not just with arms. She was restoring belief. The denial of her throne had stripped away protocol. What remained was the purpose. Lakshmibai now spoke with clarity that few had heard before. In meetings with nobles and loyalists, she did not talk of revenge—she spoke of duty. "We are not just defending stone," she told them. "We are defending the right of a child to inherit his father's legacy. The right of a people to not be bought or bartered."

She knew what was coming. Across India, sparks were beginning to fly. Discontent simmered in cantonments and princely states alike. The sepoys—Indian soldiers in the British army—were growing restless. Farmers were crushed under revenue burdens. Unfamiliar laws were reshaping ancient cities. The pressure was not only in Jhansi. It was everywhere.

By early 1857, as rumours of mutiny spread from Meerut to Awadh, the question was no longer if there would be resistance—it was when.

And Jhansi would be ready.

The British had misread Lakshmibai as a grieving widow. They did not understand that within her grief lay something far more dangerous to empire—conviction.

They expected submission.

She gave them preparation.

They expected fear.

She gave them resolve.

And when the Rebellion of 1857 finally exploded, it did not catch her unawares. It found her standing on the ramparts of Jhansi Fort, armed with not just weapons but with memory—with every letter they ignored, every insult she endured, and every promise she had made to herself and her people.

They had said no.

But she had never stopped saying yes—to justice, her child's future, and a city's unbroken will.

This chapter in Jhansi's story was not written with blood or a blade. It was written in refusals.

Refusal to disappear.

Refusal to yield.

Refusal to forget who she was and what she stood for.

When the British denied her throne, they thought they had ended her reign.

But they had only given her a reason to rise.

CHAPTER EIGHT: A QUEEN WRITES BACK

The verdict had come down like a gavel in an empty hall—final, cold, and echoing through the corridors of Jhansi.

The throne was gone. Her son dismissed. The state annexed.

But even as the banners were pulled down and her title stripped from British records, Lakshmibai did not disappear. She did not grieve publicly. She did not shout or rage at the heavens. Instead, she sat at a low writing table in the Rani Mahal, her posture composed, her thoughts sharper than any blade in her armoury.

If they believed they had silenced her, they had gravely misread their opponent. She did what few expected: she sat quietly at a table in the Rani Mahal and prepared to fight in a language the British claimed to respect—reason. This is because Lakshmibai had learned something many rulers never mastered: that a queen could command armies—but she could also command *language*. And she was about to turn every page, every letter, every clause they had thrown at her into a weapon of her own.

Thus, her first retaliation came not with a raised sword but an ink-stained hand. It was a letter—addressed directly to Lord Dalhousie, the Governor-General of India. It was written in dignified prose, not emotion, and carried the weight of constitutional clarity. She recounted the facts: the legal adoption of Damodar Rao, her husband's dying wish, the presence of a British political officer during the ceremony, and the precedent in Indian and British law that upheld such adoptions. She cited not grievances but principles. Not passion, but evidence.

This was not a queen pleading for pity. It was a head of state demanding justice.

With her royal seal affixed, the letter was dispatched to Calcutta. And then, silence. Not a single acknowledgement. No clarification. No answer. Just the Company's cold refusal, as if the voice of a queen no longer warranted even the courtesy of a reply.

But Lakshmibai would not be dismissed so easily.

She summoned the best minds she could find—vakils trained in the law, political thinkers, retired administrators, and scholars versed in British legal codes and traditional Hindu jurisprudence. With their help, she composed a second appeal. This one is more detailed, more forceful, and more pointed. She compared Jhansi's case with other annexed states like Satara and Nagpur, revealing a clear pattern of selective enforcement. The Doctrine of Lapse, she argued, was being wielded as a political weapon under the guise of legality. And worse—it violated the treaties the British had once sworn to uphold.

The letters were translated into English and Persian. Multiple copies were made and sent to Calcutta, Bombay, and Delhi. She wanted the message to echo—not just in Company offices but in the minds of every Indian ruler who might be next.

Still, no reply came.

But the silence did not stall her—it fueled her. Jhansi had lost its title, but Lakshmibai's voice was gathering power. Her correspondence spread far beyond the city. Traders whispered of her resolve. Nobles began to pay attention. The people began to understand that this was not just a queen betrayed—this was a woman building resistance word by word, law by law, page by page.

While others prepared for revolt with powder and steel, she built a legal fortification. She studied maps of the region, revenue ledgers, adoption laws, and treaties signed by her predecessors. She read British commentaries on Indian governance and highlighted every contradiction between their words and deeds. And through all of it, she kept writing.

Each letter was more precise than the last. Her arguments tightened. Her references sharpened. There was a calm fire behind every sentence. In one letter that was believed to have been addressed to Queen Victoria, Lakshmibai posed a devastating but straightforward question: "If a woman in your land can wear the crown, why is it shameful for a woman in mine to defend it?"

No one can say whether the letter ever reached Buckingham Palace, but the message was undeniable. This was no ordinary protest. It was a challenge articulated with elegance and unshakable clarity.

Meanwhile, Jhansi was transforming again. The Rani Mahal, modest by royal standards, became a quiet seat of strategy. It was not a court of opulence but of preparation. Officials began returning. Soldiers visited discreetly. Old alliances were revived. Beneath the surface of her legal campaign, Lakshmibai was building something more significant—a refusal to be erased.

She trained Damodar Rao each morning, continuing his education in scriptures and statecraft. She personally oversaw grain stores and supply chains. She interviewed soldiers, demanded updates on fort maintenance, and, in every act, reminded those around her: we are still a people, and I am still your queen.

Her words had not reversed the annexation, but they had kept her authority alive in the minds of her people. They saw a ruler who did not disappear into widowhood. They saw a woman who challenged an empire with no armies, only truth—and did not blink. And with each passing week, more voices joined her cause—quietly, steadily.

This battle of letters wasn't simply resistance. It was *memory-building*. She was inscribing her version of events into history—not letting colonial declarations define Jhansi's story but by the will of its people and the words of its queen.

And though the British still kept their silence, they watched. Reports filtered back to Company officials: the Rani had not relented. She still held court, trained, and wrote.

They had thought Jhansi had conquered. But conquest, as Lakshmibai was proving, could not be measured solely by captured land. It had to be measured by whether a people still believed in the sovereignty of their own name.

By early 1857, as the storm of rebellion was gathering across the plains of northern India, Rani Lakshmibai had become more than a widow. More than a claimant. More than a petitioner. She had become the inked resistance of an entire kingdom—the first footnote of revolution written in quiet defiance.

The Company had taken her crown. They had dismissed her heir. They had redrawn the borders of her state.

But they had not silenced her.

And when the first embers of mutiny caught fire, it was not a war cry that reached the ears of the empire—it was the echo of a woman who had written herself back into history.

CHAPTER NINE: PREPARING FOR WAR

By mid-1857, Jhansi was no longer the quiet city the British believed they had pacified. Beneath its temples and winding lanes, a transformation was taking place—silent, disciplined, and driven by a woman who had been told to accept loss as her fate.

But Lakshmibai had never believed in fate—not the kind others wrote. Her petitions had been rejected, her throne stripped, and her adopted son denied. She had waited through months of silence, studying every move the British made and every hesitation in their tone. While the East India Company believed they had ended her reign, she was building something more substantial than a crown. She was preparing for war. Not just any war. A war led by a woman fought on terms no one expected and trained in defiance of everything society had told her she could not do.

She began with her people. Quietly, steadily, she recalled the soldiers of Jhansi. Men who had once served her husband. Maratha warriors who had learned the art of combat under the Peshwas. Cavalrymen whose discipline had been buried beneath British dismissal. They returned, not for gold, but because of her—because she had stood her ground when no one else had. And she did not sit on a throne to welcome them. She was with them at dawn drills. She mounted horses with the speed and ease they remembered from her youth. She trained with the sword again and again until her arm ached. She sparred against generals and foot soldiers alike. And she never expected anything from them that she did not demand of herself.

Within weeks, her courtyard had become a place for transformation. Swords were unwrapped and sharpened, shields polished, muskets checked, oiled, and reassembled, and blacksmiths called back into royal service. Old weapons buried after the annexation were uncovered and restored. She did not allow wasted movements. Every strike, step, and command had a purpose. Lakshmibai understood that she would not win through size—her forces would always be outnumbered. She would win through precision, speed, and belief. But to fight the British, she first had to fight a more profound enemy: expectation.

Widows were meant to wear white, to fade into ritual silence. Queens without thrones were expected to retire with dignity. Women were not taught to give orders to generals. And certainly not to lead battalions.

She defied every one of those roles.

She wore armour.

She spoke in council chambers.

She ordered weapons.

She invited women—yes, women—into her military ranks. Not to cook or clean but to fight.

Her announcement was simple and without flourish: "If our homes are threatened, let those who defend them learn to do so with their own hands."

And the women came. Some were daughters of merchants, some were widows of soldiers, and some had never touched a weapon. She trained them personally, sword in hand and bow drawn. They ran drills in hidden fields outside the city. She taught them to ride, move silently, and stand without flinching. To those who questioned her, she replied only: “If they attack us, do you expect me to ask the British to wait while our men return?” Even her closest advisors—loyal Maratha nobles and older court ministers—looked at her with awe and concern. But they knew better than to object. She was not breaking the rules to shock them. She was breaking the rules because they were built to make her lose.

As the days grew hotter, so did the preparation. Jhansi Fort, ancient and sprawling, was examined wall by wall. Guards were posted. New gates were reinforced. Supplies—grain, water, cloth, and medicinal herbs—were stockpiled in underground chambers.

From her rooftop, at night, she could see torches lighting up the training grounds. Young men sparred, their movements reflected in the flames. Older men stood watch, crossbows in hand. Occasionally, she would descend silently and join them, catching their mistakes before they realized she was there.

They called her “Rani-saheba” to her face. But among themselves, she was becoming something more: commander, guardian, Jhansi’s shield.

She met secretly with messengers from other princely states. Some had already joined the rebellion, and some were watching, waiting to see who would rise. Lakshmibai gave them no slogans, no speeches, only facts. She showed them her soldiers, her rebuilt fort, and her plans.

And her eyes.

Because more than her words, it was her presence that convinced them. This was not desperation. This was deliberate defiance.

Intelligence began to arrive from the north. Cities falling. British cantonments under siege. Whole regiments defecting. And yet, still, Jhansi had not been attacked. The Company watched warily. They assumed that Rani would bide her time.

But she wasn't waiting.

She was choosing her moment.

Each morning, she drilled her army. Each afternoon, she read reports. And each evening, she walked the fort ramparts with her son beside her, pointing out where to look, where to post archers, where the walls were strongest—and where they must be made more substantial.

She trained him not just in movement but in meaning.

He was a child of no official name or recognized title.

But to her, he was her son, her heir, and one day, perhaps, her successor in courage.

When some British agents questioned her preparations, she responded with customary calm: "A queen without a throne may still need walls to protect her people."

But she was doing far more than building walls.

She was building the expectation of resistance.

Hope had taken root among her people—not that victory was assured, but dignity was possible. That surrender was not the only option. That someone, at last, was willing to face death on their behalf and not from behind a veil.

By late summer, her army was no longer a theory.

It was a force.

Still small, outgunned—but disciplined, united, and led by someone who refused to submit had become a legend.

She did not promise triumph.

But she was preparing for it.

And when the day came—and it would come—that the Company returned to enforce its law with fire, they would find more than a city.

They would find a queen at the gates.

Not waiting.

But ready.

She had no throne, but she commanded loyalty.

She wore no crown, but her word was law.

She did not inherit power—she created it.

What Lakshmibai forged in those months was not just an army. It was a message to her people, her enemies, and history that the queen of Jhansi was not waiting for approval, rescue, or permission. She was ready to defend what others had already declared lost.

Every sunrise brought new drills, and every night, new decisions. But beneath the sweat and steel was something more profound—a quiet fire that no sword could extinguish. She was training a city not just to fight but to believe it deserved survival, to lead, to rule itself.

She had crossed the boundaries drawn for her by culture, gender, and empire—and never looked back.

So when the sound of war finally reached Jhansi, she would not be caught unprepared. The gates would be manned. The walls would hold. And at the centre of it all would be a woman who had rewritten every expectation laid at her feet.

Not because she wanted to fight.

But because she would never allow herself—or her people—to be conquered quietly.

CHAPTER TEN: THE 1857 REVOLT

She had not wanted to fight.

But she would never allow herself—or her people—to be conquered quietly.

By May of 1857, that promise would become prophecy. Across northern India, fires had been lit—not just in streets and barracks but in the minds of those who had long been silenced. The rebellion, born in mutiny, was swelling into something far more extensive: a reckoning. And when it reached the gates of Jhansi, it did not find a city asleep. It found a city already standing.

Lakshmibai had spent months preparing—not for rebellion, but for self-defence. Her soldiers were trained. Her weapons sharpened. Her spirit, already tested by betrayal, was now ready for battle. Yet, even as the uprising spread, she remained measured. Jhansi had not yet declared open war. She waited—listening, watching, calculating.

That changed with a single shot.

On June 5, 1857, mutinous sepoys from the British garrison in Jhansi revolted. They stormed the cantonment, seized the treasury, and killed British officers and their families. The uprising had reached her doorstep. But Lakshmibai had not ordered it—and she would not allow chaos to take control of her city.

When the bloodshed ended, Jhansi was leaderless. The sepoys, without command structure or plan, prepared to flee. But the city, its people, its children—they needed protection. The citizens of Jhansi turned to the only person they trusted. And they did not knock quietly. They demanded her return to power.

At first, she resisted.

She had been wronged, yes—but she had not joined the killings. She had hoped still that some semblance of justice might be recovered. But the British had made no distinction. Even as she tried to restore order, even as she sent letters to Calcutta pleading her innocence in the massacre, they dismissed her as complicit.

They did not investigate. They condemned.

And just like that, every hope of diplomacy was gone.

So she stepped forward—not as a usurper, but as a protector. She resumed control of the city, reestablished the guard, protected British prisoners still alive, and restored stability. But the message from the Empire was already clear: Lakshmibai was an enemy.

And if they saw her as one, she would become one on her terms.

It was now war.

The months that followed were relentless. The British, regrouping from uprisings across the country, began their march back toward Bundelkhand. Jhansi was marked for retribution.

Lakshmibai transformed into a wartime leader with unshakable clarity. The city became a fortress. Grain was rationed. Weapons were redistributed. Every wall was reinforced. She spent her days on horseback, inspecting trenches, speaking to generals, and comforting women who feared for their families. At night, she studied tactics by lamplight, examining siege histories and the formations of British infantry.

She was not only preparing for battle—she was preparing to be remembered.

The British response came in March 1858. Sir Hugh Rose, leading a well-trained force of British troops and Indian allies, surrounded Jhansi. They expected a swift campaign and believed the city, led by a woman, would fall within days.

It lasted nearly two weeks.

Lakshmibai commanded her troops from the front. She rode in full armour through the heart of battle, encouraging, directing, and defending. When cannon fire breached a portion of the southern wall, she rallied her cavalry personally, pushing the attackers back before they could penetrate further. She issued daily orders, negotiated local alliances, and kept morale burning even as food dwindled and the wounded mounted.

Inside the fort, children carried arrows, women boiled oil, and civilians learned to throw stones, light torches, and guard doors. This was not just a battle for territory; it was a siege for identity.

But the British had numbers, artillery, and time. On April 3, after days of bombardment, they breached the walls. The final assault was brutal. Buildings burned. Fighters fell. The city trembled. But Lakshmibai refused to surrender.

With her adopted son Damodar Rao strapped to her back, she mounted her horse and led a final breakout charge through a narrow gate in the fort's rear. Fewer than twenty riders made it out alive.

But she was one of them.

So, the story that might have ended in a conquered city became the beginning of a living legend.

She did not stop riding.

From Jhansi, she rode to Kalpi, where rebel forces regrouped. There, she met other leaders of the uprising—Tatya Tope, Rao Sahib, and others. She was no longer just the Rani of a lost kingdom. She had become the face of resistance itself. They attempted to organize a new front to unite scattered regiments under one command.

In Kalpi, she fought again. When defeat came, she moved once more, this time toward Gwalior. The rulers there wavered—first refusing, then surrendering the city to rebel forces as the British advanced. But Lakshmibai did not pause. She raised the independence flag at the Gwalior fort and declared that their fight was over.

Her enemies pursued. The pressure tightened. But her courage only grew.

The final battle took place in June 1858 near the town of Kotah-ki-Serai, outside Gwalior. Lakshmibai led her cavalry directly into the

British line. She fought not like royalty but like a soldier—fierce, agile, and focused.

She was shot from her horse.

Accounts vary—some say she was killed instantly, others that she was wounded and asked a follower to take her away so her body would not be defiled. But all accounts agree on this: she died with her weapon drawn.

And she died as she had lived.

Not asking for peace.

But proving that freedom could be fought for.

Even when the odds were impossible.

Even when the world said no.

Even when every rule told her to bow her head.

As we know, she had no army left, no city to return to, her fort occupied, and her allies scattered. But what remained—what could never be taken—was the way she had stood, fought, and refused, again and again, to be anything less than sovereign over her own story.

Even in death, she commanded reverence. The British, stunned by the ferocity of her final stand, buried her with respect. Their reports called her "the best and bravest of all rebel leaders." It was not praise—

it was acknowledgment—a reluctant salute to a woman they could not break.

But her most incredible legacy was not written in British records or rebel chronicles. It lived in the silence that followed her fall—in the pause between what had ended and what had been awakened. Because after Lakshmibai, something had shifted. A curtain had been pulled back. An example had been set.

A woman, uninvited to the halls of policy or the tables of Empire, had changed the shape of a rebellion.

She had not waited to be named a hero. She had acted like one.

And by doing so, she showed every man, woman, and child who watched her ride through Jhansi's streets or charge into open fields that resistance was not a privilege. It was a duty. It was not a performance. It was a presence. It was not granted. It was taken.

Not all battles are fought to be won. Some are fought so the world cannot pretend it did not see.

And the world saw her.

It saw a woman wrapped in armour instead of ashes. It saw a mother who carried her child into war not as a shield but as a reason. It saw a ruler who answered the collapse of her world with strategy, conviction, and the unwavering will to protect those who called her queen.

The rebellion would be suppressed. The Empire would recover. Jhansi would fall.

But she would not be forgotten.

Because even in retreat, even in defeat, Lakshmibai had forced the Empire to confront something it could never rule:

A woman who had decided for herself what it meant to be free.

CHAPTER ELEVEN: THE LAST STAND

The British had taken her palace, her title, and her land. They had hunted her across rivers and plains. They had circled her name in official reports, determined to end the rebellion by capturing or killing its fiercest symbol. But Lakshmibai was not a symbol they could contain.

She was the fire their empire had failed to extinguish. And now, in the searing heat of June 1858, after months of evasion, defiance, and impossible survival, she stood not as a fugitive but as a commander. Her city had been seized. Her forces were dwindling. But the woman they thought they had broken had returned to the battlefield stronger than ever. This was no longer resistance. This was her last stand, for Lakshmibai was not a woman built from what she had. She was shaped by what she refused to surrender.

After the fall of Jhansi, she rode not into retreat but into resistance. At Kalpi, she regrouped with Tatya Tope and other rebel commanders. Exhausted, injured, and hunted, she could have stopped there. No one would have blamed her. But she did not. She still had strength, and as long as her people were still being pursued, that strength was not hers to keep—it belonged to them.

From Kalpi, they moved to Gwalior. The city's rulers faltered, caught in a tightening vice between loyalty to the British and fear of the rebels. And Lakshmibai, ever decisive, did not ask for their permission. She and her forces entered Gwalior, raised the flag of rebellion above the fort, and declared the city free.

For a moment, it felt as if history might bend.

But the British were already on the march. With a disciplined force and a memory of humiliation at Jhansi, Sir Hugh Rose moved quickly to retake what had been claimed. He did not underestimate her anymore. This was not about one city or one queen. It was about ensuring that no one, anywhere, thought they could challenge the empire and survive.

Lakshmibai knew this would be her final stand. She made no speeches and had no illusions. But she would not die in retreat, unseen, or as a memory. She would become something they could never erase.

On the morning of June 17, 1858, outside the city near a place called Kotah-ki-Serai, the British and rebel forces clashed. The air was thick with dust and fire. Lakshmibai, dressed in a soldier's uniform, rode into the chaos with her adopted son tied to her back for protection. She had trained for this. Her entire life had led to this moment—not to die but to show what it meant to live for something more than fear.

She fought in the thick of the battle. British officers later wrote that she fought with skill and fury that defied every expectation. A queen, they had thought. But they saw a warrior, commanding, striking, never once falling back.

There are many stories about how she died. Some say she was shot. Others say she was wounded and asked a soldier to help her off the battlefield so her body wouldn't fall into British hands. A few claimed she was cremated by a local family who honoured her last request. History leaves room for doubt. But no one doubts this: she fought until the very end.

When her body was gone, her story only grew.

Even her enemies could not deny her valour. Usually cold and clinical, British reports described her as "the bravest and best of the rebel leaders." That was not flattery. That was fear speaking in the voice of respect.

In the days that followed, British troops reoccupied Gwalior. They pressed forward. They marked victories on maps. But something had changed. Everywhere they went, her name had gone before them—not just as a fighter, but as a fire—something no amount of rifles or policies could bury.

What she had started in Jhansi was no longer about her. It was in the women who stood taller because they had seen what she dared to do. It was in the soldiers who remembered her riding through smoke like thunder on horseback. It was in the rebels who, even in defeat, knew they had not knelt.

Lakshmibai did not live to see freedom. But she became the measure of it.

She had no kingdom left to defend. No walls to protect. No crown to wear. But what she chose to defend in her final moments was something far more enduring. She stood for the right to resist. To be heard. To lead, not because she was allowed to but because she refused to be silent. Her death did not end her story—it began a legacy. The British may have taken her city, but they could not erase the image of the woman who rode into battle with a child at her back and fire in her heart.

Even her enemies could not deny what they had seen. In their official records, they called her brave. In their private reports, they called her dangerous. In truth, she was both. What she left behind was not a rebellion but a reminder—that strength wears many faces and courage doesn't ask for permission. She had rewritten what leadership could look like, what resistance could feel like, what history could remember.

In the years to come, her name would echo through classrooms and battlefield songs, whispered in revolts and shouted in parades. Not as a myth. As a fact. As the woman who dared. She did not live to see a free India, but she lived precisely as one would expect its first true daughter of independence to live: boldly, without fear, and with no intention of being forgotten.

CHAPTER TWELVE: WHY YOU'LL NEVER FORGET HER

When I began writing this book, I had no idea what it would become. I just knew I had questions. Why don't we study the women who influenced history? Why do some names shine while others fade? Why does Rani Lakshmibai, who defied empires, led armies, and stood taller than most kings, only get a few lines in our textbooks? Looking further, I discovered someone who changed how I saw the world and myself, even though I wasn't searching for a hero. What started as research evolved into an awakening. She wasn't just a queen from the past. Her voice reverberated into my present. I invite you to join me on this journey of discovery, to explore the contributions of women in history and to evaluate their applicability today.

Since we are told we can be anything but are still evaluated based on our speech, appearance, dreams, and even how we sit, I am being raised in a disorganised time. We are reprimanded for being "too bold" or "too loud," but we are exhorted to take the lead. Despite being surrounded by technology and drenched with viewpoints, we are fundamentally still searching for our place in the world. Today, being a girl repeatedly feels like navigating a world designed to challenge, scrutinize, and occasionally erase you. There's always pressure to look good, prove yourself, and keep quiet to maintain harmony. And you're accused of being demanding when you attempt to break those patterns. Dramatic. Too much. Not enough. It gets tiring—this silent war of just being.

Which is why Rani Lakshmibai is important to me. She did not ask permission. She did not wait to prepare. She took what life offered her—loss, injustice, betrayal—and created purpose out of it. She was a woman who lived in an age when women were not even given a voice in courtrooms, and she led from the front. She made decisions that kings would be too scared to take. She did not fight because she loved war. She fought because she felt her people were worth more. She did not wish to be a warrior. But the world gave her no choice. This is why she is impossible to forget—not her wars, but her courage to rise repeatedly when all around her was telling her to quit. In a world that measured women by their silence, she roared.

Today, I see how much we still require Rani Lakshmibai. Girls are still taught to sit when they need to stand up for themselves. Women are still being taught to make uncountable amendments to make others comfortable. We still exist in a world where a girl's achievement is extraordinary rather than ordinary. We witness girls battered, dismissed, or silenced for being too loud. Powerful women are being attacked not for what they say but for the way they say it. Even in this new age of so-called progress, we carry the burden of having to prove ourselves repeatedly. That's why Lakshmibai isn't just history—she is prophecy. She's the standard we point to when we're lost when we think small, and when we need to be reminded that we are allowed to fight for ourselves and those who cannot. But we are not alone in this fight. We are part of a more significant movement and can bring about the change we seek together.

I sometimes wonder what she would say to girls like me. Girls are learning to live in their bodies while carrying the world's expectations as they navigate friendships and futures. She may have explained to us that bravery is not synonymous with fearlessness. She might serve as a reminder that remaining gentle can be a sign of strength in a cruel world. Or perhaps, like the warrior she was, she would stand by us in silence and let her story speak: You don't need to be flawless to be strong. You must not give up. Her life serves as a reminder that authority is not dependent on consent. Sometimes, history doesn't remember the loudest—it remembers the ones who refused to disappear.

Writing this book has changed more than how I see the past. It has altered my self-perception. I once believed that to make a difference, I needed to mature and understand my voice had to be earned. Lakshmibai, however, didn't wait. Her grief, her age, and her gender did not deter her. By refusing to let others write her story, she created it herself. I now remember that lesson whenever I stood up in class, defended someone, or wrote something that seemed too important for someone my age to write. I carry her with me always.

You might not have a sword or a castle to protect. But you have something just as substantial—your honesty. Your words. Your power to say, "I'm worth more." This is what Lakshmibai left for us. It's a gift of standing up and a guide to live with meaning, self-respect, and strength. We'll never forget her—not because she was flawless or legendary—but because she was genuine—a woman who walked into history and made a spot no one could take. And because of that, she's already made a spot in us, in every girl who decides to stand tall and in every woman who chooses not to back down. In every person who believes that no matter who you are, your life story is important.

Maybe someday, when someone asks about my childhood hero, I won't just name Rani Lakshmibai. I'll smile and say, "She taught me to become my hero." Heroes don't always wear capes or win medals. Sometimes, they remind us that courage doesn't mean fearlessness, that our words count even when we stutter, and that our inner spark can light the path even in dark times.

Rani Laxmibai didn't just motivate me to study history—she sparked my desire to shape it. She boosted my confidence to enter rooms as I belong, speak like I deserve attention, and stand proud—not because I know everything, but because I no longer seek permission to be myself.

I want every woman labelled as excessive to recall that excess is what transforms the world. And I wish anyone who's ever felt scared to stand up thinks of Rani Lakshmibai—standing up repeatedly even when everything knocked her down. She's part of all of us now. In each brave act. In each minor revolt. In each quiet choice, keep pushing forward.

And that's why we'll never forget her.

Because we are her legacy.

CHAPTER THIRTEEN: THE SURPRISING BITS

History is usually served in straight lines: dates, battles, speeches, and victories. But real lives are messier—and way more fascinating. Rani Lakshmibai is remembered for her bravery and brilliance, but beyond the headlines and textbooks, her life was filled with unexpected details, strange coincidences, and stories that don't always get told in classrooms. This chapter is for those stories. The surprising bits. The things that made me stop say, "Wait—really?" and smile a little bigger.

Let's start with her name. She was born Manikarnika Tambe, but her nickname at home was Manu. The name "Lakshmibai" came later—after her marriage to the Maharaja of Jhansi. And yes, she took the name "Lakshmi" from the Hindu goddess of prosperity, but also because it matched the court traditions. So, the fearless queen we know? She started as "Manu," a girl who climbed trees, practised sword fighting, and refused to sit still in a sari.

One of the coolest facts I found? She trained her horse to respond to different whistles. Lakshmibai's favourite horse was named Badal, and according to some accounts, she could leap onto him from the back of another galloping horse. During the British siege of Jhansi, it's believed she escaped through a narrow gate with her child tied to her back—while riding Badal, who jumped from the fort wall. Sadly, the horse didn't survive the leap, but it helped save a queen and her future.

She also had a unique fighting style. Many British officers described it with surprise, sometimes even admiration. Unlike other royal women who stayed behind palace doors, Lakshmibai wore soldier's armour and joined the cavalry. She often carried two swords—one in each hand—and could fight ambidextrously. That means she was just as strong with her left hand as with her right. In a battle. On a horse. While leading an army. At twenty-something years old. Let that sink in.

Another twist? She wasn't originally planning to lead a rebellion. She tried diplomacy. She wrote calm, legal letters. She appealed to the British sense of justice. Her goal wasn't violence—it was fairness. She only turned to arms after being repeatedly denied her rights, ignored, and insulted. The Rani who rode into battle didn't want war. But she refused to accept being erased.

Oh, and here's something funny: the British gave her a backhanded compliment after her death. In an official report, one general described her as "the best and bravest of all the rebel leaders." They didn't usually admit that kind of thing. But even they knew—this wasn't an ordinary opponent. She was smarter, faster, and more focused than many of the men they faced. They feared her. And they respected her.

She also inspired myth-making that still lives on today. Some stories say she disappeared after the war and lived in disguise. Others say she ascended into the heavens. While these legends might not be historically accurate, they show how deeply people believed in her spirit—that she couldn't be broken or truly defeated. For many Indians, she wasn't just a historical figure. She became a symbol, a spark, a living idea.

Here's one of my favourite surprising bits: even decades later, women across India invoked her name in protest, in poetry, and in revolutions. The most famous poem, written by Subhadra Kumari Chauhan, begins: "Khoob ladi mardani, woh to Jhansi wali Rani thi"—"She fought like a man, that queen of Jhansi." But honestly? She didn't fight like a man. She fought like herself.

Today, you'll find her statue in almost every major Indian city—usually on horseback, sword raised, child strapped behind her. She's on postage stamps, in museums, on murals, in movies. She even has roads and schools named after her. But behind every monument is a girl who once just wanted to ride horses, read books, and be taken seriously.

And maybe the biggest surprise of all? She was younger than most of us imagined. She was around 29 when she died, not much older than someone just finishing college. She did all this before most of us even figured out who we were. That doesn't make her story sad. It makes it stunning. In less than thirty years, she lived a life of such strength, passion, and fearlessness that people still talk about her 160+ years later.

And now, the Really Surprising Bits you won't always find in textbooks:

- **She May Have Had a Pet Cobra**—Oral legends in Bundelkhand say Manu wasn't afraid of snakes and even kept a cobra as a playmate. This is impossible to prove but unforgettable to imagine.

- **Her Horse Could Leap Fort Walls** – Badal was no ordinary horse. Lakshmibai supposedly trained him to leap from fort walls during emergencies—like the one that helped her escape the siege.

- **Swordplay at Age 8** – She began training alongside palace guards and boys, sneaking into sessions dressed like them. She didn't ask to be included—she insisted.

- **She Wrote Her Legal Petitions** – In Sanskrit and Persian, she argued her case to the British regarding Damodar Rao's right to the throne. Many of the letters were in her hand.

- **She Signed as "Mother of Jhansi"**—not Queen but a Mother. She saw her kingdom as a family—something to nurture, defend, and sacrifice for.

- **She Rode Barefoot into Battle** – Some say it was a vow. Others say it gave her a better grip. Either way, she faced war without armour for her feet.

- **Minimalist Style, Maximum Impact**—Despite being a queen, she wore simple cotton or silk saris with minimal jewellery—even at royal functions. She preferred grace over glamour.

- **She Reinforced Secret Escape Tunnels** – Jhansi Fort had tunnels for the royal family and civilians. She strengthened them for women's and children's safety—long before the war began.
- **She Acted and Wrote Poetry** – As a teenager, she played Sita in palace plays and was known for powerful dialogue. Her poetry is mostly lost—but the impact is not.
- **Her Final Words Were for Her Son** – As she lay dying, her last words, according to a follower, were: "Take care of my child." That's the kind of leader she was—even at the end.

She wasn't just a warrior in history—she was a wonder in every way. And the more you learn about her, the more unforgettable she becomes.

CHAPTER FOURTEEN: GLOSSARY

This glossary provides straightforward definitions for words that appear in the book. Each word helps bring the story closer, clearer, and more alive for every reader.

« **Abandoned (adjective)**

Meaning: Deserted or left behind; no longer supported or claimed.

Synonyms: deserted, forsaken, discarded
Antonyms: retained, cherished, supported
Origin: From Old French *abandoner*, from Latin *ab* ("away") + *dare* ("to give").

« **Accomplished (adjective)**
Meaning: Highly skilled or successful in a particular area.
Synonyms: proficient, talented, expert
Antonyms: inexperienced, unskilled, amateur
Origin: From Latin *complere*, meaning "to complete or fulfill."

« **Acuter (adjective - comparative)**
Meaning: More intense, sharp, or severe in degree or perception.
Synonyms: sharper, keener, more severe
Antonyms: milder, duller, blunter
Origin: From Latin *acutus*, meaning "sharp, pointed."

« **Alignment (noun)**
Meaning: Proper arrangement or positioning; agreement or alliance.
Synonyms: positioning, order, arrangement
Antonyms: disorder, disarray, misalignment
Origin: From Old French *aligner*, based on *ligne*, meaning "line."

« **Annex (verb)**
Meaning: To incorporate a territory or land into a larger political entity.
Synonyms: seize, occupy, appropriate
Antonyms: relinquish, surrender, detach
Origin: From Latin *annexare*, meaning "to tie or bind to."

« **Anticipated (verb)**
Meaning: Expected or looked forward to in advance.
Synonyms: awaited, predicted, foreseen
Antonyms: unexpected, unforeseen, surprising
Origin: From Latin *anticipare*, meaning "to take before."

« **Arrogant (adjective)**
Meaning: Having an exaggerated sense of one's importance or abilities.
Synonyms: conceited, haughty, egotistical
Antonyms: humble, modest, unassuming
Origin: From Latin *arrogare*, meaning "to claim for oneself."

« **Condemned (verb)**
Meaning: Declared to be wrong or guilty; sentenced to punishment.
Synonyms: convicted, denounced, doomed
Antonyms: acquitted, praised, exonerated
Origin: From Latin *condemnare*, from *damnare*, meaning "to inflict loss or damage."

« **Conjecture (noun)**
Meaning: An opinion or conclusion based on incomplete information.
Synonyms: speculation, guess, hypothesis
Antonyms: fact, certainty, proof
Origin: From Latin *conicere*, meaning "to throw together."

« **Contemporary (adjective)**
Meaning: Belonging to or occurring in the present time.
Synonyms: modern, current, up-to-date

Antonyms: outdated, old-fashioned, ancient

Origin: From Latin *contemporarius*, from *com-* ("with") + *temporarius* ("of time").

« **Controversy (noun)**

Meaning: Prolonged public disagreement or heated discussion.

Synonyms: dispute, debate, argument

Antonyms: agreement, consensus, harmony

Origin: From Latin *controversia*, from *contra* ("against") + *vertere* ("to turn").

« **Coronet (noun)**

Meaning: A small or lesser crown worn by nobles or royalty.

Synonyms: circlet, tiara, crown

Antonyms: —

Origin: From Latin *corona*, meaning "crown."

« **Dawned (verb)**

Meaning: Became visible or understood; began to appear.

Synonyms: emerged, appeared, began

Antonyms: faded, ended, disappeared

Origin: From Old English *dagian*, meaning "to become day."

« **Demure (adjective)**

Meaning: Quiet, modest, or reserved in manner or behavior.

Synonyms: modest, shy, unassuming

Antonyms: bold, assertive, outspoken

Origin: From Anglo-French *demurer*, meaning "to delay," later influenced by *murus* ("wall").

« **Diminish (verb)**

Meaning: To make or become less in size, importance, or value.

Synonyms: decrease, reduce, lessen

Antonyms: increase, enhance, enlarge

Origin: From Latin *diminuere*, meaning "to make smaller."

« **Endure (verb)**
Meaning: To suffer patiently or remain in existence through difficulty.
Synonyms: withstand, tolerate, persevere
Antonyms: surrender, quit, collapse
Origin: From Latin *indurare*, meaning "to harden."

« **Exposure (noun)**
Meaning: The state of being exposed to something harmful or revealing.
Synonyms: vulnerability, contact, revelation
Antonyms: protection, shelter, concealment
Origin: From Latin *exponere*, meaning "to set forth."

« **Gentle on the tongue (phrase)**
Meaning: Smooth, mild, or pleasant in taste or speech.
Synonyms: soothing, mild, palatable
Antonyms: harsh, bitter, offensive
Origin: Figurative usage combining "gentle" (Latin *gentilis*) and "tongue" (Old English *tunge*).

« **Glossing (verb)**
Meaning: Explaining something, often superficially; disguising or smoothing over.
Synonyms: explaining, skimming, sugarcoating
Antonyms: revealing, exposing, clarifying
Origin: From Greek *glossa*, meaning "tongue" or "language."

« **Hitherto (adverb)**
Meaning: Until now or up to this time.
Synonyms: so far, until now, thus far
Antonyms: afterward, henceforth
Origin: From Old English *hider to*, meaning "to here."

« **Hoofbeats (noun)**
Meaning: The sound made by a horse's hooves striking the ground.

Synonyms: clopping, thudding, galloping
Antonyms: silence
Origin: Compound of "hoof" (Old English *hof*) + "beat."

« **Inducing (verb)**
Meaning: Persuading or causing someone to do something.
Synonyms: prompting, encouraging, influencing
Antonyms: deterring, discouraging
Origin: From Latin *inducere*, meaning "to lead in."

« **Interpretive (adjective)**
Meaning: Providing or related to explanation or meaning.
Synonyms: explanatory, illustrative, analytical
Antonyms: ambiguous, confusing
Origin: From Latin *interpretari*, meaning "to explain."

« **Invigorated (verb)**
Meaning: Filled with energy or strength.
Synonyms: energized, refreshed, revitalized
Antonyms: drained, exhausted, weakened
Origin: From Latin *vigere*, meaning "to be lively."

« **Languidly (adverb)**
Meaning: In a slow, relaxed, or weak manner.
Synonyms: sluggishly, lazily, faintly
Antonyms: energetically, briskly
Origin: From Latin *languere*, meaning "to be faint or weary."

« **Manipulation (noun)**
Meaning: Skillful or unfair control or influence.
Synonyms: control, exploitation, influence
Antonyms: honesty, openness, fairness
Origin: From Latin *manipulus*, meaning "a handful."

« **Marksmanship (noun)**

Meaning: Skill in shooting or aiming with precision.
Synonyms: sharpshooting, accuracy, gunnery
Antonyms: inaccuracy, clumsiness
Origin: From *marksman* (one who hits a target) + *-ship* (denoting skill).

« **Moderation (noun)**

Meaning: Avoidance of excess; balance and restraint.
Synonyms: temperance, self-control, balance
Antonyms: excess, extremism, overindulgence
Origin: From Latin *moderatio*, from *moderari*, meaning "to control."

« **Nationalist (noun)**

Meaning: A person strongly devoted to promoting national interests.
Synonyms: patriot, loyalist
Antonyms: internationalist, globalist
Origin: From French *nationaliste*, based on Latin *natio*, "nation."

« **Nestled (verb)**

Meaning: Settled or placed snugly or comfortably.
Synonyms: snuggled, tucked, nestled
Antonyms: exposed, uncovered
Origin: From Middle English *nestlen*, from *nest*.

« **Obscurity (noun)**

Meaning: The state of being unknown, inconspicuous, or difficult to understand.
Synonyms: anonymity, vagueness, ambiguity
Antonyms: clarity, fame, prominence
Origin: From Latin *obscuritas*, from *obscurus*, meaning "dark."

« **Omens (noun)**

Meaning: Signs or events believed to predict the future.
Synonyms: portents, warnings, signs

Antonyms: surprises, coincidences
Origin: From Latin *omen*, meaning "foreboding or prophetic sign."

« **Pantheon (noun)**
Meaning: A group of particularly respected people or deities.
Synonyms: icons, legends, gods
Antonyms: unknowns, mortals
Origin: From Greek *pantheion*, meaning "temple of all gods."

« **Perspective (noun)**
Meaning: A particular way of viewing something; point of view.
Synonyms: viewpoint, outlook, stance
Antonyms: narrow-mindedness, bias
Origin: From Latin *perspectiva*, meaning "to look through."

« **Piety (noun)**
Meaning: Religious devotion and reverence.
Synonyms: devotion, holiness, faith
Antonyms: irreverence, impiety
Origin: From Latin *pietas*, meaning "dutifulness, religiousness."

« **Pondered (verb)**
Meaning: Thought deeply or carefully about something.
Synonyms: considered, contemplated, reflected
Antonyms: ignored, disregarded
Origin: From Latin *ponderare*, meaning "to weigh or consider."

« **Pounding (noun/verb)**
Meaning: A series of heavy or loud blows or beats.
Synonyms: thumping, hammering, beating
Antonyms: tapping, silence
Origin: From Old English *punian*, meaning "to crush."

« **Prophesied (verb)**
Meaning: Predicted or foretold a future event.
Synonyms: predicted, foretold, forecasted

Antonyms: ignored, withheld
Origin: From Greek *prophēteuein*, meaning "to speak for, foretell."

« **Pulsating (adjective/verb)**
Meaning: Throbbing or vibrating with a rhythmic beat.
Synonyms: throbbing, beating, quivering
Antonyms: still, motionless
Origin: From Latin *pulsare*, frequentative of *pellere*, "to strike."

« **Quivering (verb/adjective)**
Meaning: Trembling or shaking with slight motion.
Synonyms: trembling, shivering, shaking
Antonyms: steady, still
Origin: From Middle English *quiveren*, likely of Germanic origin.

« **Rebellion (noun)**
Meaning: Resistance or defiance against authority or control.
Synonyms: uprising, revolt, insurrection
Antonyms: obedience, submission
Origin: From Latin *rebellio*, from *rebellis*, meaning "waging war again."

« **Reeked (verb)**
Meaning: Emitted a strong or unpleasant smell.
Synonyms: stank, smelled, emanated
Antonyms: fragranced, perfumed
Origin: From Old English *reocan*, meaning "to emit smoke."

« **Remnant (noun)**
Meaning: A small remaining quantity or piece.
Synonyms: leftover, residue, fragment
Antonyms: whole, entirety
Origin: From Latin *remanere*, meaning "to remain."

« **Robust (adjective)**
Meaning: Strong, healthy, and full of energy.

Synonyms: sturdy, vigorous, resilient
Antonyms: weak, fragile, frail
Origin: From Latin *robustus*, from *robur*, "oak, strength."

« **Romanticized (verb)**
Meaning: Presented in an idealized or unrealistic way.
Synonyms: idealized, glorified, dramatized
Antonyms: downplayed, deglamorized, realistic
Origin: From Latin *romanticus*, relating to fiction and emotional expression.

« **Rupture (noun/verb)**
Meaning: A sudden break or burst; a split in relations.
Synonyms: break, split, fracture
Antonyms: connection, unity, repair
Origin: From Latin *ruptura*, from *rumpere*, meaning "to break."

« **Savvy (noun/adjective)**
Meaning: Practical knowledge and understanding; shrewdness.
Synonyms: cleverness, insight, know-how
Antonyms: ignorance, cluelessness
Origin: Possibly from Spanish *sabe* ("he knows"), from Latin *sapere* ("to be wise").

« **Smouldering (verb/adjective)**
Meaning: Burning slowly without flame; showing suppressed emotion.
Synonyms: glowing, simmering, seething
Antonyms: blazing, extinguished
Origin: From Middle English *smolderen*, meaning "to smother."

« **Splendour (noun)**
Meaning: Magnificent and impressive appearance or quality.
Synonyms: grandeur, magnificence, brilliance
Antonyms: dullness, modesty, plainness
Origin: From Latin *splendor*, meaning "brightness."

« **Stripped (verb)**
Meaning: Removed coverings or possessions from something.
Synonyms: uncovered, peeled, deprived
Antonyms: clothed, adorned, covered
Origin: From Old English *strypan*, meaning "to plunder."

« **Subcontinent's (possessive noun)**
Meaning: Belonging to a large, distinct region of a continent.
Synonyms: region's, area's, territory's
Antonyms: continent's
Origin: From Latin *sub-* ("under") + *continentem*, "continent."

« **Submission (noun)**
Meaning: The act of yielding to authority or control.
Synonyms: surrender, compliance, obedience
Antonyms: resistance, defiance
Origin: From Latin *submittere*, meaning "to let down, yield."

« **Testament (noun)**
Meaning: Something that serves as proof or evidence; a formal statement.
Synonyms: evidence, tribute, declaration
Antonyms: denial, contradiction
Origin: From Latin *testamentum*, meaning "a will, declaration."

« **Treaties (noun)**
Meaning: Formal agreements between states or organizations.
Synonyms: agreements, pacts, accords
Antonyms: conflicts, disputes
Origin: From Latin *tractatus*, from *tractare*, meaning "to handle."

« **Treaty (noun)**
Meaning: A formally concluded agreement between countries.
Synonyms: accord, contract, deal

Antonyms: breach, quarrel
Origin: From Old French *tretet*, from Latin *tractatus*.

« **Tyranny (noun)**
Meaning: Cruel and oppressive rule or government.
Synonyms: dictatorship, oppression, despotism
Antonyms: democracy, freedom, justice
Origin: From Greek *tyrannos*, meaning "absolute ruler."

« **Unconventional (adjective)**
Meaning: Not based on or conforming to accepted rules or standards.
Synonyms: unusual, original, nontraditional
Antonyms: conventional, typical, standard
Origin: From Latin *convenire* ("to come together") + prefix *un-* ("not").

« **Unwavering (adjective)**
Meaning: Steady, firm, and resolute.
Synonyms: firm, steadfast, unflinching
Antonyms: wavering, uncertain, indecisive
Origin: From *un-* ("not") + *waver*, from Middle English *waveren*.

« **Violated (verb)**
Meaning: Broke or failed to comply with a rule or agreement.
Synonyms: breached, infringed, desecrated
Antonyms: respected, upheld, obeyed
Origin: From Latin *violare*, meaning "to do violence to."

« **Wary (adjective)**
Meaning: Cautious or alert to danger or problems.
Synonyms: cautious, vigilant, guarded
Antonyms: careless, reckless, trusting
Origin: From Old English *wær*, meaning "prudent, aware."

« **Wearied (verb/adjective)**
Meaning: Tired or exhausted, especially from effort or exertion.
Synonyms: fatigued, drained, worn out

Antonyms: energized, refreshed, invigorated
Origin: From Old English *werig*, meaning "tired."

CHAPTER FIFTEEN: WHERE I FOUND MY FACTS

I searched all the sources of truth: books, people and websites. This book is a story of struggle, realisation, and personal growth, as reflected in the diverse range of portals I utilised to obtain information.

It wasn't always simple. I would occasionally hit a dead end or experience a hassle in tracking the information down. I had to be uncompromising and stoic. But I never gave up, thanks to the encouragement from my parents. They helped me find books that I couldn't locate at school and taught me how to use the Internet to search effectively. Their counsel to take one step at a time was palliative when information overload left me feeling overwhelmed. Their role in my journey was crucial, underscoring the importance of parental support in any endeavour.

Likewise, my grandmother wasn't just a significant influence on me; she ignited my passion for history. Her tales about the past, full of vivid details, helped me connect with the subject and made me fall in love with it. She was instrumental in helping me identify and nurture my willingness to explore unchartered territories—like a little archaeologist spying through every book, article, or chat to uncover hidden information. Whether it was in a distracting online article, a note from a teacher, or an old history book, I loved the exhilaration of spotting small facts that others might have overlooked.

I began by flipping through the pages of my history textbooks, paying particular attention to chapters such as "The Making of the National Movement" and "Colonialism and the City" in my NCERT History for

Class 8 course. I then went to the school library and checked out books by Romila Thapar, such as "Ancient India," and Ramachandra Guha, including "India After Gandhi."

At school, I used Chromebooks to access Google Scholar, JSTOR, and The Hindu Archives, digging through academic articles and newspaper clippings. I spoke to my history teacher, Mr/Ms_________________________, and asked for advice. She/He shared his sources, such as the National Digital Library of India (NDLI) and Cambridge History resources, and even let me review his PowerPoint presentations for additional insights.

I also revisited notes and materials from my past projects, like my research on Mughal architecture, which reminded me of how much I enjoy uncovering facts about India's rich history. I cross-referenced everything with online resources, including www.britannica.com, indiaculture.gov.in, and the National Museum of India's digital exhibits.

Every resource I used, including articles and library books, helped me gain a more comprehensive understanding of the subject. As a historical explorer, it was more than just gathering data; it was about making connections, exercising critical thought, and following my intuition. My project ultimately captures not only what I learnt but also the path I took to get there, which was full of obstacles, curiosity, family support, and a lifelong love of learning.

My grandma used to say, "You don't just learn history; you experience it through the stories you unearth." Throughout my initiative, I kept thinking about those words of wisdom. They served as a reminder that every piece of information I discovered was part of a bigger story that was waiting to be told, not just a detail in a book. This project wasn't only about gathering data, which is why I termed it "My Journey to the Truth." It involved questioning what I discovered, venturing into the unknown, and putting everything together like a jigsaw. In retrospect, I see how much this experience has shaped who I am. I've learned patience, critical thinking, and the delight of exploration from it. I now see history as a living narrative that moulds who we are rather than merely a subject we study in school. I've come to realise that education is an adventure, thanks to this project, and I'm eager to learn more.

References:

1. Guha, Ramachandra. *India After Gandhi: The History of the World's Largest Democracy.*

2. Thapar, Romila. *Ancient India.*

3. Nehru, Jawaharlal. *The Discovery of India.*

4. NCERT. *History for Class 8* and *Themes in Indian History (Class 12).*

5. Singh, Upinder. "Urbanization in Ancient India." JSTOR.

6. EPW. "Trade and Commerce in Ancient India." Economic and Political Weekly, 2001.

7. Britannica. *www.britannica.com*.

8. Indiaculture.gov.in.

9. National Museum of India Digital Exhibits.

10. The Hindu Archives and History Today articles.

11. Asher, Catherine. *Mughal Architecture of India*.

12. British Library Online Archives.

13. National Digital Library of India (NDLI).

14. The Times of India Historical Archives.

Verses Kindler Publication

erses Kindler

ublication

Verses Kindler Publication

Reach us through our website -

https://www.verseskindlerpublication.com/

For more information visit our Instagram or Facebook page.